BOOKS BY MARJORIE KINNAN RAWLINGS

The
Secret River

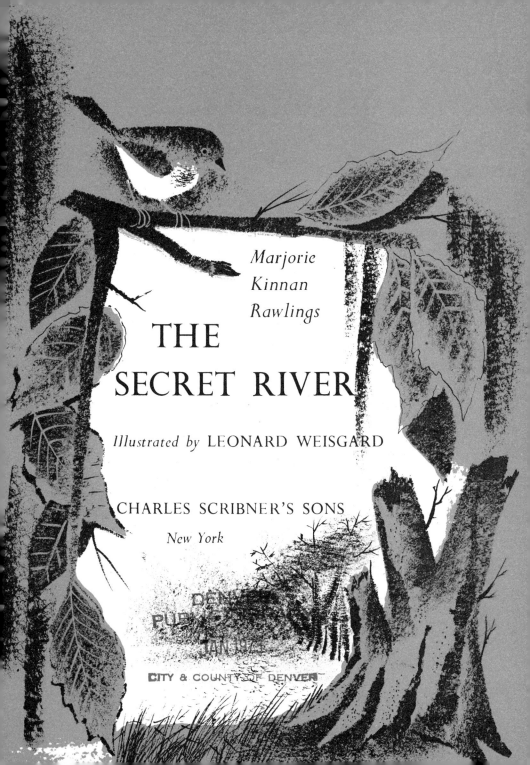

Marjorie
Kinnan
Rawlings

THE
SECRET RIVER

Illustrated by LEONARD WEISGARD

CHARLES SCRIBNER'S SONS
New York

G330396

H-6.72(AJ)

JR 199 se

SBN 684-13119-6(R B, Cloth)
Library of Congress Catalog Card
No. 55-6916

INTRODUCTION

The Secret River is the only finished work that has turned up so far among the papers left by Marjorie Kinnan Rawlings. While it has for background her beloved Florida, which was the setting of most of her writing, it is quite different in style from her other work and is the only children's story she wrote. It may be of interest, therefore, to tell something of what we know about it.

From the letters between the author and her great friend and editor Maxwell Perkins we learn that one reason it was not published earlier was that the author had some feeling that Calpurnia and her story if left to themselves might develop into a longer book. Mr. Perkins seemed to share her hope. There is no indication that either of them was dissatisfied with the story as it was; in fact Mr. Perkins spoke warmly of its "quality of enchantment."

To the question posed to the reader, is Calpurnia's secret river *real*, Maxwell Perkins made this lovely answer: "Now the way I am looking at the story is that the things in the story actually happened, but that it did not seem to Calpurnia that they were as they were. For one thing, she was a little child. Everyone as a child can remember coming upon some seemingly enchanted spot of incredible beauty, and a sort of unreality, where for the time everything was perfect and right. That does not only happen to a child either, but an adult does not believe actually in the magic of it. I remember for one instance, climbing up the cliffs beside a waterfall as a boy, and coming to the top where the brook had spread out almost into a little river and flowed peacefully, and the green meadows on each side. It was like entering fairyland. Everyone knows about this. I would have it that the adult reader would so understand, and yet you would have all the latitude you wanted. The bear and the panther could be thought of as almost imagined by Calpurnia. In this interpretation, Mother Albirtha might presumably have given the advice, 'Follow your nose,' thinking the girl knew where she was and would soon get home, and then when she did turn up with the fish and Mother Albirtha said she would never see the river again, it would signify to the adult that she realized that this child had been through one of those magical experiences, and that while she might have others, this one would never recur. The river would never look to her as it had that time, even if she did see it again."

Marjorie Kinnan Rawlings' untimely death brought to an end any imagined book which might have grown from this story. But surely we can be happy to have *The Secret River* as it is here, for it is in itself complete and charming.

Julia Scribner Bigham

The
Secret River

There is a dark green forest far away in Florida. The trees are so tall that the sky is like a blue veil over their leafy hair. Vines with red and yellow flowers grow up the trees. Red and blue and white and gray birds have their nests in the branches. Squirrels scamper up and down the trunks, and bury their acorns and their hickory nuts among the roots. At night, when there is no one but the owls to see, small animals with soft fur and bright eyes run and play and hunt for their supper.

There is a path through the forest. It leads to the home of Calpurnia and Buggyhorse.

Calpurnia is a little girl and Buggy-horse is her dog. Her name is Calpurnia because she was born to be a poet. Buggy-horse is a peculiar name, but even when he was a puppy his back dipped in the middle and he had an enormously fat stomach, just like a little old buggy-horse. He could not possibly have been called Rex or Rover or any ordinary name for a dog. Calpurnia wrote her first poem about him:

My dog's name is Buggy-horse
Of course.

On the morning when this story begins, Calpurnia was awakened very early. Outside her window, two red-birds were singing to each other. They sang so loud that

she heard them in her sleep, and she woke up. She listened, and she decided that one red-bird was singing, "Love me? Love me? Love me?" and the other red-bird was singing, "Sure do. Sure do. Sure do." The red-birds flew away together to build a nest. Calpurnia looked over the side of her bed. Buggy-horse was still sound asleep on his own hooked rug beside her bed.

She said to him, "Wake up, my dear dog. I have a feeling something special is going to happen today."

Buggy-horse just stretched himself and yawned. He was a lazy dog. He liked to sleep for hours and hours, sometimes in the sunshine and sometimes in the shade.

He hoped Calpurnia was not getting ready for an adventure. He was obliged to follow her wherever she went, because he was miserable when she was out of his sight.

Calpurnia washed her face and hands and brushed her teeth and combed her hair. Because of her feeling, she put on her best pink hair-ribbons. She made her bed neatly. Her room was so clean and tidy that company could have come at any moment.

She went out-of-doors with Buggy-horse and saw that it was indeed a beautiful day. The sun was shining and the oranges on the trees were as bright as balls of gold. She said a poem.

Lovely day,
Come what may.
If I did not love
    my mother
        and my father
I would run away.
Because
    it is a running-away
Kind of day.

As it turned out, she had the best reason in the world for making a journey.

Her mother called, "You two little hungry things, come and get your breakfast."

At breakfast, Calpurnia's father said, "Hard times have come to the forest."

She said, "What are hard times?"

"It means that everything is hard, and especially for poor people."

She felt of the table, she laid her hand on Buggy-horse's back, she ate another mouthful of grits, and it was true, everything seemed harder than usual.

She asked, "Are we poor people? I don't feel poor."

Her father said, "We are poor people. I make an honest living selling fish to other poor people. Now there are no fish. Nobody can catch any fish. I shall have to close my fish market and things will go hard with all of us."

Calpurnia ate her hard grits and patted Buggy-horse's hard back and she said a poem.

I wish
We had fish.
Then hard times would end.
But I am not the least little bit worried,
    because
Everybody be's my friend.

Her mother said, "You can't say 'every-body be's my friend.' It sounds as if you're talking about bees. Honey-bees or bumble-bees."

Calpurnia was delighted. She changed her poem in her mind and then she said:

Everybody's bees is my friends.
Everybody's flowers is my flowers.
Everybody's happy hours
    is my happy hours.
All this goes on
    and there is no ends.

"That's better," said her mother. "You are really a smart child. But you should say, 'are' no ends."

So Calpurnia said, "Are no ends. Are, are, are," and Buggy-horse said, "Arf, arf, arf."

Her mother said, "I sometimes don't know who's the smartest, you or that little old Buggy-horse dog."

Her father said, "It won't matter who's the smartest, if I can't get fish to sell to the other poor people," and he went to his empty fish market.

Calpurnia went outside and stood beside a tree and thought about the fish market. There was a small pond where she and Buggy-horse often went to fish, but

she had never caught anything there except tiny minnows. Also, she used angleworms for bait, and they were squirmy and had to be kept in a glass jar. She did not like this and she imagined that the angleworms did not like it, either.

But my, she did love to go fishing. She did not know which she loved best, Buggy-horse, or fishing, or making poems.

She said to herself, "Now if I was a fish, what would I like to bite?"

She thought and thought, and she had a wonderful idea.

She said to Buggy-horse, "If I was a fish, I would only bite something unusual and something pretty."

She went up a ladder on the outside of the house, that led to the attic.

She remembered some beautiful pink crepe paper, left over from a birthday party.

Buggy-horse tried to follow her up the ladder, but he was so fat in the stomach that

he had to give up. She came down again with the pink paper, she found a pair of scissors, and she went to her mother.

"Mother dear, may I make some pink paper roses?"

"Of course, my child."

Her mother was very considerate and did not ask questions unless she had to. So Calpurnia made some large roses from the pink paper and tied them to the ends of her pig-tails. She set out with Buggy-horse and her fishing pole to find Mother Albirtha, who was the wisest person in the forest. Mother Albirtha was sitting in front of her little shop. She was worried about hard times, too, like Calpurnia's father, for if there are no fish, and one person is poor, then everybody else is poor, too, and Mother Albirtha had no customers at all.

Calpurnia said, "Mother Albirtha, I am going fishing, to keep my father from being poor. I have fished in the pond, but the fish there are so small. You are the wisest person in the forest. Will you tell me where I can catch some big fish, so that hard times will be soft times?"

Mother Albirtha rocked back and forth.

She said, "Child, I have not breathed this to a living soul, but I will tell you. There are big fish in the secret river. Oh my, the fish! Catfish, perch, bream, mudfish and garfish. Especially catfish."

"Is the secret river far away?"

"Nobody knows. I will tell you this— you will be home again by nightfall."

"How will I find it?"

"Just follow your nose. You will know the river when you see it."

"Thank you, Mother Albirtha. When I catch the fish, I will bring you some."

"Child, you talk like an angel."

Now Calpurnia thought it was foolish to find anything by following her nose.

She said to Buggy-horse, "My nose goes straight ahead. How will I know where to turn?"

But she started out into the forest. The first thing she knew, a rabbit hopped by. She turned to look at him, which meant that her nose pointed to the right. So she followed her nose. After a while, a blue-jay flew into a live-oak tree and scolded her for running away. She turned her nose

to the left, to look at him. So she followed her nose. All of a sudden, she heard a sound like music. The forest had ended. Calpurnia had found the secret river. The river was so beautiful that she sat down on a cypress knee to admire it. The cypress

trees were sitting at the edge of the water
to cool themselves. Their bony knees stuck
out of it.

She said to the cypress trees, "I hope
you don't mind if I sit on one of your
knees to admire the secret river."

The cypresses clicked their green needles, which she took for permission. The river was singing as it ran by. Then she saw the fish. They were jumping and dancing, and there were so many of them that they got in each other's way.

Calpurnia said to the fish, "Do you mind if I catch some of you, to save the forest from hard times?"

The fish did not answer, so she took that for permission, too. Now she saw a little red boat tied to the bank. It had a sign on it. The sign said:

"Please tie me up again when you are through with me. I am so afraid of getting lost."

Calpurnia stepped into the red boat with her fishing pole and the pink paper roses tied to her pig-tails. Buggy-horse followed her into the boat. She pushed away from the shore. The boat rocked gently on the river. She took one of the pink paper roses from her braids and tied it to the hook on the end of her fishing line. The pink rose floated for a few minutes, and then sank slowly down through the water. An old frog sitting on the bottom of the river saw it.

He croaked, "Now what in the water is that thing? It's meant to catch fish, that's what it is. Well, I won't bite it, that's sure."

He settled himself to watch, and before he had blinked his eyes, a huge catfish tried to swallow the pink paper rose, and was hauled out of the river on the end of Calpurnia's fishing line.

The old frog grunted, "I knew it. There is nothing more foolish than a fish."

Sitting in the red boat, Calpurnia pulled in one fish after another. Buggy-horse hung over the side in excitement. Just as Mother Albirtha had promised, there were more catfish than anything else, and this pleased

Calpurnia for two reasons. In the first place, the people in the forest dearly loved to eat catfish, and her father could get a higher price for them. In the second place, catfish are extremely disagreeable and try to stick everybody with the sharp barbs on their heads. Calpurnia thought that fish who go out of their way to stick people deserve to be caught.

After a while, Calpurnia had as many catfish in the red boat as she could possibly carry home. She pushed the boat in to the shore and tied it carefully to the trunk of a cypress tree. She moved the fish to the ground and Buggy-horse helped her. He could only carry one fish in his mouth at a time, but he worked hard and did his best.

Calpurnia said to him, "How can we carry all these fish home?"

Buggy-horse looked at the fishing pole and barked. He looked at a clump of bear-grass and barked. Calpurnia understood at once. Bear-grass has long, thin, tough leaves, and they can be used like strong pieces of string. She broke off the leaves and passed them through the gills of the fish, and tied the fish on the fishing pole. She put the pole over her shoulder. It was very heavy with all the catfish on it.

She started out for home. It was late afternoon, and shadows were already falling through the forest.

She said to Buggy-horse, "Mother Albirtha told us to find the secret river by following my nose. Do you think we can get home the same way?"

Buggy-horse barked, and she decided to try to get home the same way. A gray fox turned her nose to the left, and a mother raccoon with two baby raccoons turned her nose to the right. It was getting dark. The sun had set, the day animals were going to bed and the night animals were coming out to play and hunt for their supper. Calpurnia heard a strange sound.

A deep voice called, "Who-o-o-o? Why-y-y-y? Who?"

Calpurnia did not know where the ques-
tions came from, but she answered bravely,
"I'm Calpurnia. Who are you?"
The voice said, "Who-o-o-o."
"Why, it's just a hoot-owl."

But then she saw the hoot-owl sitting in the top of a dead tree. He was enormous and he did not look friendly. She wondered if he had come out to hunt for his supper. He rolled his big round eyes at her fish. He rolled his big round eyes at Buggy-horse. No doubt about it, he was very hungry.

Calpurnia said quickly, "Please, Mister Hoot-owl, can I give you a nice fresh cat-fish for your supper?"

The hoot-owl cocked his head on one side and flapped his wings. He flew down into a small wild plum tree beside her. It was a great deal of trouble to untie the cat-fish from the fishing pole, but she picked out the biggest fish of all and laid it on the clean grass. The hoot-owl swooped down and began eating it at once, without saying "Thank you."

She said, "You are welcome anyway," and she and Buggy-horse went on.

The forest was so dark she could not see her nose in front of her face, so of course she could not follow her nose.

"I'm not a bit worried," she said out loud.

She was really worried, but she said it to cheer up Buggy-horse.

All of a sudden she saw a huge black shadow in front of her. The shadow moved and Buggy-horse growled.

Calpurnia thought up a poem quickly.
She called out:

Shadow, shadow, go away.
You wouldn't scare me in the day.
I won't be scared because it's night.
Shadow, shadow, be polite.

The shadow was a big black bear. Calpurnia's heart went thump-thump-thump. Buggy-horse tried to hide behind the catfish.

Calpurnia thought, "Maybe the bear is hungry, too."

She said in a small frightened voice, "Mister Bear, could I interest you in a nice fresh catfish for your supper?"

The bear snuffled as if he needed a handkerchief and he came closer. She did not wait to pick out the biggest catfish. She pulled two from the fishing pole as fast as possible and laid them on the clean grass. She did not run away, but she hurried. She called over her shoulder, "You're entirely welcome," in case the bear had thanked her. Buggy-horse did not say a word. He was really scared. The forest was as black as a bear.

Then Calpurnia saw something crouching ahead of her. It was a panther. She did not know whether he was friendly or unfriendly, but she thought, "I'm sure he's hungry. I expect hard times have even come to the panthers in the forest."

So she said, "Mister Panther, you are a sort of cat, and cats love fish, and I should like to give you some nice fresh catfish for your supper."

She was not so frightened now, and she took three catfish from her fishing pole and laid them on the clean grass.

The panther began eating them at once, and he purred so loudly that she knew he was saying "Thank you."

She said, "You are certainly most welcome."

She said a poem:

If somebody scares you, the thing to do
Is give somebody something to.
Then they never bother you.
Sometimes they say "Thank you."

Calpurnia and Buggy-horse went on, although they could not see their way. And then the full moon rose and the forest was as bright as day. She smelled night-flowers blooming. Calpurnia said a poem:

> The night
> Is bright
> With white moonlight.
> The little things
> Have songs
> and wings.

A mocking-bird began to sing in the moonlight. The night birds began to fly. A white crane flew straight across the moon. It dropped a white feather and Calpurnia picked it up and tucked it in her hair.

And then she saw that they were out of the forest, and on the path home. Buggy-horse barked joyfully and ran ahead.

Calpurnia said, "It would be nice to go home this minute, but I promised Mother Albirtha some fish. So come, my dear dog."

Mother Albirtha was just turning out the light in her shop when she heard the knock on her door.

"Who is that, knocking so late?" she called.

"It is Calpurnia, with your fish."

Mother Albirtha's eyes were as big as saucers when she saw the fish.

"Child, where did you catch all those catfish?"

"Why, in the secret river, where you told me to go."

"Oh my goodness to the may-haw bush. I forgot all about what I told you. Oh my goodness to the swamp maple."

Calpurnia was busily untying the fish from the fishing pole.

"How many catfish do you want, Mother Albirtha?" she asked.

"Oh my goodness to the red-bud tree. Just give me one catfish, child. Just one nice fat catfish."

Calpurnia chose the nicest and fattest and Mother Albirtha wrapped it in her apron. They all said "Good night," and Calpurnia and Buggy-horse hurried on home. All the lamps were burning in the

house. Calpurnia's mother and father put their arms around her and began to cry.

"Dear daughter, we thought you were lost in the forest."

"Oh, no. I just followed my nose. And see, I brought fish to turn hard times to soft times. I gave some away, but it was necessary."

Her mother and father could not believe their eyes when they saw the catfish.

"Child, how did you catch all these

fish? How did you carry them home by yourself? Where have you been?"

But Calpurnia was so tired and so sleepy that she could not answer. She drank a cup of cocoa and her mother undressed her and tucked her into bed and Buggy-horse lay down to sleep on the hooked rug beside her. She did not know another thing until it was morning. Her father had gone to his market to sell the catfish.

A man who had not had anything to eat for a long time bought the first catfish. He said he would pay for it as soon as he had eaten it and had earned money for a day's work, for he had been too weak from hunger to work. A woman who had not had anything to eat for a long time bought the second catfish, and said she would pay for it as soon as she had eaten it and earned money for a day's work, for she had been too weak from hunger to work. All the people from the forest bought the catfish and ate them and felt strong again and went out into the world and found work to do. They earned money, and that night they all paid Calpurnia's father for the catfish, and had money to spare. Mother Albirtha had six customers in her shop. Calpurnia's father had a big pile of money. And so hard times in the forest turned to soft times.

One day Calpurnia and Buggy-horse started out to find the secret river again. They searched all that day, and all the next day, and the next. Calpurnia followed her nose this way and that way. She found strange flowers and strange birds and strange little pools of water. But she could not find the river. So she went to Mother Albirtha.

"Mother Albirtha," she said, "I cannot find the secret river."

Mother Albirtha rocked back and forth.

"Child," she said, "this is a sad thing to tell you. There is not any secret river."

"But Mother Albirtha, you told me how to find it, and I found it. I want to find it again."

Mother Albirtha rocked back and forth.

She said, "Child, sometimes a thing happens once, and does not ever happen any more."

Calpurnia said, "But I want to catch more catfish in the river."

Mother Albirtha said, "Child, you caught catfish when catfish were needed. Hard times have turned to soft times. So you will not find that river again. I told you once, and I tell you twice, there is not any secret river."

"But I saw it. It must be somewhere for I caught fish there."

Mother Albirtha rocked back and forth.

"The secret river is in your mind," she said. "You can go there any time you want to. In your mind. Close your eyes, and you will see it."

Calpurnia was delighted. She skipped all the way home. Buggy-horse chased his peculiar tail.

Calpurnia sat down under a magnolia tree and closed her eyes.

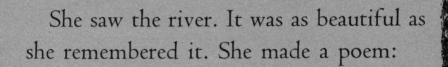

She saw the river. It was as beautiful as
she remembered it. She made a poem:

The secret river is in my mind.
I can go there any time.
Everything Mother Albirtha says is true.
The sky is gold and the river is blue.
River, river, I love you.

She opened her eyes, and the river was gone. She felt sad. She did want to see it again with her eyes open. She knew that it was truly somewhere in the forest. Some day, she would find it once more. It probably ran straight out into the world. The world, she was sure, was a kind and beautiful place. She said another poem:

The world is full of love.
It sings like a turtle dove.
The world will love me
And under a cypress tree,
On its knee,
We will watch the secret river together.
We will find a white bird's feather.

Calpurnia pulled an orange from the tree beside the gate. She threw it like a ball for Buggy-horse to play with. He brought it back to her at last, and then she ate it.